Shosu
Mistake

Written by John Lockyer
Illustrated by Vanessa Eunson

Rigby

THE FIRST CONTACT

Palo hurried along the track. Far away he heard Dax yell at the dogs. He ran even faster. He didn't know where he was going; he just knew he had to hurry. He followed the path into the trees and slowed to a walk. Then he saw the silvery orb and remembered why he had come.

He was looking for the cows when he had first seen the orb. He had been afraid. He wanted to run away, but his legs wouldn't move. Some strange force held him – a force from the orb. When the force let him go, he had turned and raced down the hill. He jumped over fences and ditches and skidded around the barn, crashing into Dax. The dogs barked and Dax shouted. Palo tried to remember where he had been.

Each day some force drew Palo to the woods. When he returned, Dax would be waiting. "Where have you been, Palo?" he would ask. Palo tried to tell him, but couldn't. His memory was blank.

"You are up to mischief, Palo!" Dax would say.

Palo stared at the orb. Today it was different. It seemed to glow and flash. He tried to move on down the path. Nothing. His legs would not move. Then a door opened in the side of the orb. Palo put his arms over his head and hid his eyes. He heard a voice inside his head. Peeking through his arms, he saw a strange creature emerge from the orb. The voice came again. "Don't be afraid. I will not harm you."

5

SHOSUN'S MESSAGE

Palo dropped his arm. The voice started again – inside his head. A mind message.

"I am Shosun," said the voice. "Come. There is something you need to see."

Palo's head spun. Everything became a blur. When he opened his eyes, Shosun and the orb were beside him, but the land that he knew had gone.

"We have mind-traveled to Planet Gallo," said Shosun. "Gallo is a small planet, just like Earth, but it is in a different solar system."

Palo looked at the land around them. The trees and grass were dead. An oozy black liquid covered everything. Palo moved his feet. The black ooze squelched and sucked at them.

"The black ooze is a virus," said Shosun. "It is killing the land. I was sent from Planet Nasco to get samples of the virus. We must find a vaccine."

Palo looked at Shosun. He didn't understand. He felt afraid. He wanted Dax.

Shosun seemed to sense his fear. "I was on my way home to Nasco," he said, "when the orb broke down. I was drawn into Earth's orbit. I had to land and fix the orb, but . . ."

Palo had to speak. "What do you want?" he cried. "Why am I here?"

Shosun's words rang inside his head. "Look around you. Look at the land! Look at the ooze! You had to see it!"

"Why?" shouted Palo. "Why?"

"Because the same virus is now on Earth."

Palo felt weak. He didn't want his farm to be covered with black ooze. He shook his head. "How?" he asked. "How did this virus get to Earth?"

Shosun was quiet. Then he said, "It came with me. That's why I want to help. That's why you have to help me."

"Me?" said Palo.

"Yes. I will take samples of the virus back to Nasco. Our laboratories will make a vaccine. I will send the vaccine back to Earth on an orb. It will be programmed to land in the woods. You must check for the orb every day."

Palo nodded. He felt stunned.

"Every day," Shosun repeated. "Do you understand? You must destroy the virus with the vaccine or it will destroy Earth."

Again, Palo nodded. "Please," he said. "Let me go home."

Palo's head began to whirl. He felt himself spinning in a blur of glowing light. When the spinning stopped he heard Shosun's voice. Palo opened his eyes. He was floating high above Earth.

"Look down there!" said Shosun. "The trees and grass are yellow. They will soon die. The ooze is already here. It is smothering their roots."

Palo looked at the fields. Shosun was right. The fields were turning yellow. Suddenly he felt dizzy. He was spinning, tumbling, falling . . . . As he spun, he heard the words over and over: "Shosun's mistake . . . Shosun's mistake . . . mistake . . . ."

Something . . . Somewhere?

When Palo's head stopped spinning, he found himself under a small tree. He felt something wet and rough on his face. It was one of the dogs licking him. He pushed it away and saw Dax coming up the path. "Get down to the barn," said Dax. "There are cows to be milked."

Palo got to his feet. "Dax . . .?" he said.

But Dax had stomped off. Palo chased him. Suddenly he stopped and touched the back of his shirt. It was wet. He walked back to the tree. He saw a thick black ooze seeping from the bark. Palo scratched his head. He knew it wasn't a fungi. It was something else. Something he had seen somewhere . . .

WHAT IS SCIENCE FICTION?

Science Fiction is a narrative in which the author uses scientific language and ideas to write about an imaginary futuristic world.

A science-fiction story has a plot with:

| A Problem | An Introduction | A Resolution |

HOW TO WRITE A SCIENCE-FICTION STORY

STEP 1 Make a *story plan* to help you organize your story.

Introduction

Who		Event
Where	→	Event	→	Problem	→
When		Event

Event	
Event	→ Resolution

STEP 2

Look back at your plan and write an *introduction*, using:
– *characters* from the future
– a *setting* in a futuristic imaginary world
– *scientific words*: orb, force, etc.

STEP 3

Write about the *events* of the story that led up to the *problem*.

STEP 4

Write about *what happens* as a *result* of the events, i.e., the *problem*.

STEP 5

Write about the *sequence of events* that led to the *resolution*.

STEP 6

Write about the *resolution*. Tell the reader *how* the problem was resolved.

Guide Notes

Title: Shosun's Mistake
Stage: Fluency (4)

Text Form: Science Fiction
Approach: Guided Reading
Processes: Thinking Critically, Exploring Language, Processing Information
Written and Visual Focus: Chapter Heads

THINKING CRITICALLY
(sample questions)
- How can you tell this is a science-fiction story?
- Why do you think Palo's memory was blank? Why couldn't he tell Dax where he had been?
- What do you think was meant by the words "Shosun's Mistake"?
- How do you feel about the ending of the story?

EXPLORING LANGUAGE

Terminology
Spread, author, illustrator, credits, imprint information, ISBN number

Vocabulary
Clarify: orb, force, emerge, blur, solar, ooze, virus, vaccine, squelched, laboratories, programmed, smothering, seeping, fungi
Pronouns: he, you, I, him, it, we
Adjectives: *silvery* orb, *strange* creature, *oozy black* liquid
Homonyms: seen/scene, weak/week
Antonyms: remember/forget, rough/smooth, different/same
Synonyms: destroy/ruin, peeking/peeping, stunned/shocked

Print Conventions
Hyphen: mind-traveled
Apostrophe – possessive (Shosun's Mistake, Earth's orbit, Palo's head)